To my dear friends Margarita Londoño,
Fabio and Marcela, Enrique Lara, Jairo Buitrago,
Carlos Riaño and everyone from Sancocho.

Gusti

This Poop Is Mine!
Somos8 Series

© Text and Illustrations: Gusti, 2020
© Edition: NubeOcho, 2020
© Translation: Cecilia Ross, 2020
www.nubeocho.com · hello@nubeocho.com

Original title: *¡Esta caca es mía!*
Text editing: Rebecca Packard

First edition: 2020
ISBN: 978-84-17673-88-8
Legal Deposit: M-38211-2019

Printed in Portugal.

THIS POOP IS MINE!

Written and illustrated by Gusti

One day, just as he did
every other morning,
George went out into the garden
and left a little present.

George couldn't suspect the terrible chain of events
his little present would unleash…

Just as she did every other morning, Lola,
a very flitty fly, went out to buzz around
and stretch her wings. Without even batting
an eye, she came to land at the top of the
enormous steaming mountain.

With the triumphal air of a conquering
heroine, she planted her flag.

"I, Lola, the flittiest of all flies,
do hereby declare: This poop is mine!"

Lola's life was now perfect, magnificent, complete, marvelous.

"I'm so happy!" she exclaimed.

She was so happy that she didn't notice another fly approaching, this one with decidedly unfriendly intentions.

This new fly buzzed around a couple of times and then landed.
She looked from side to side and then said, dripping with disdain,

"I, Fiona, the laziest and most loudmouthed of all flies,
do hereby declare: This poop is mine!"

"No way!" said Lola. "I was here first, and it's mine!"

"Oh, phooey!" exclaimed Fiona angrily. "This poop is—"
KERSPLAT! She hadn't even finished her sentence when
a big fat ball of poo hit her right in the face.

"If it's a war you're after, then that's what you'll get!"
Fiona shouted.

The two flies started stomping their feet in the mire,
while flapping their wings full tilt with a deafening buzz.

That's the way flies declare war.
The great battle had begun.

Lola and Fiona used all
their cunning and skill.

There could be only one victor.

They were so busy fighting,
they didn't realize the sun
had begun to set.

Now, as everyone knows, flies love sleeping, so they agreed to a ceasefire. They drew a white line down the middle of the poop, so that neither of them could cross over to the other one's side during the night.

The hours ticked by, and the two flies continued their untrusting vigil. What if the other one decided to step over the line and break the pact?

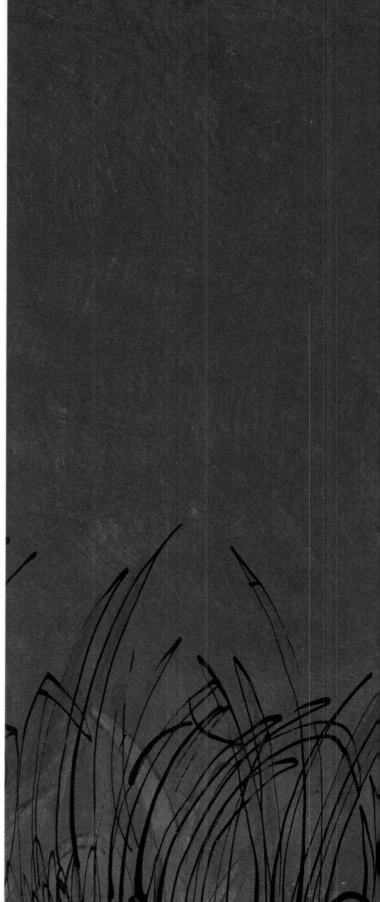

When the sun rose again, Lola and Fiona were so tired, they had no more energy left to keep on fighting. And they realized that there was, after all, plenty of room for the both of them.

Suddenly, the earth began to shake.
A gigantic shadow fell over the poop.

Just as he did every other morning,
Peter the gardener went out into
the garden to water the flowers.

Lola and Fiona ended up lying together… in the hospital!

In the end, they became close friends, and they promised that next time, they would say…

THIS POOP
IS OURS!

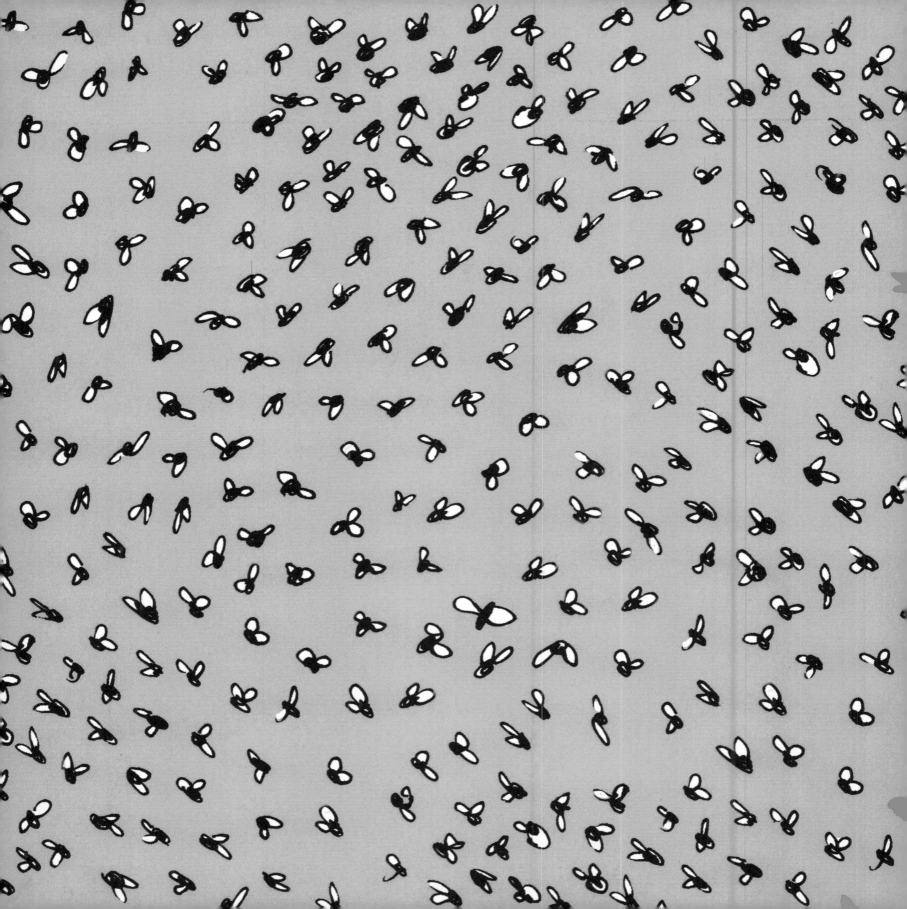